For
Gabriel

First US edition 2022

Library of Congress Catalog Card Number 2021946701
ISBN 978-1-5362-2425-2

21 22 23 24 25 26 APS 10 9 8 7 6 5 4 3 2 1

Printed in Humen, Dongguan, China

This book was typeset in Futura and hand-lettered by the author.
The illustrations were done in gouache.

Candlewick Press
99 Dover Street
Somerville, Massachusetts 02144

www.candlewick.com

CANDLEWICK PRESS

A Good Place

Lucy Cousins

Four insect friends were looking
for a good place to live.

I want **leaves,**
said Ladybug.

I want **flowers,**

said Bee.

I want dead
Wood,

said Beetle.

I want a pond,

said Dragonfly.

Soon the friends found some beautiful flowers.

Maybe this is a good place to live, said Bee.

But the flowers were
growing on a busy sidewalk.

Then the insects found a tiny pond.

maybe this is a good place,
said Dragonfly.

But the pond was just a dirty puddle
on a noisy road.

Oh no!
This is NOT
a good place.

Soon they found some dead wood.

Hooray! said Beetle.

Maybe this is a good place.

But the dead wood was in a smelly pile of garbage.

Look,

said Ladybug.

Some gorgeous green leaves. Maybe this is a good place.

But someone came and
sprayed the leaves.

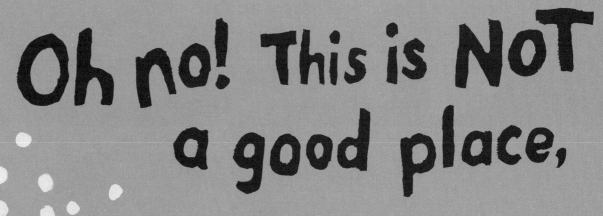

Oh no! This is NOT
a good place,

said the insects,
coughing and spluttering.

The four friends felt hungry
and sick and tired.

Maybe we will never find a good place,

said Ladybug, starting to cry.

But then they heard a fluttering . . .

It was a lovely butterfly.

Hello, little insects.
What's wrong? she said.

We can't find a
good place to live.

Butterfly smiled.

I can help you.
Come with me and look
over this wall.

WOW!
said the four friends.

It's wonderful.

The boy who lives here loves insects and he has made his garden a good place,

said Butterfly.

There were flowers for Bee, leaves for Ladybug,

a pond
for Dragonfly—
but where
was Beetle?

Here I am,

said Beetle, laying eggs
in this dead wood.

At last we have found
A GOOD PLACE!